DK READERS

BEGINNING TO READ ALONE **2**

John Cena

Written by Brian Shields

DK Publishing

The scene was *WrestleMania 21*
in 2005. John Cena lifted his
opponent over his head. Then he

A Note to Parents

DK READERS is a compelling program for beginning readers, designed in conjunction with leading literacy experts, including Dr. Linda Gambrell, Professor of Education at Clemson University. Dr. Gambrell has served as President of the National Reading Conference, the College Reading Association, and the International Reading Association.

Beautiful illustrations and superb full-color photographs combine with engaging, easy-to-read stories to offer a fresh approach to each subject in the series. Each DK READER is guaranteed to capture a child's interest while developing his or her reading skills, general knowledge, and love of reading.

The five levels of DK READERS are aimed at different reading abilities, enabling you to choose the books that are exactly right for your child:

Pre-level 1: Learning to read
Level 1: Beginning to read
Level 2: Beginning to read alone
Level 3: Reading alone
Level 4: Proficient readers

The "normal" age at which a child begins to read can be anywhere from three to eight years old. Adult participation through the lower levels is very helpful for providing encouragement, discussing storylines, and sounding out unfamiliar words.

No matter which level you select, you can be sure that you are helping your child learn to read, then read to learn!

LONDON, NEW YORK, MUNICH,
MELBOURNE, AND DELHI

For DK/Brady Games
Publisher David Waybright
Editor-in-chief H. Leigh Davis
Licensing Director Mike Degler
International Translations Brian Saliba
Director of Business Development
Michael Vaccaro
Title Manager Tim Fitzpatrick

Reading Consultant
Linda B. Gambrell, Ph.D.

Produced by
Shoreline Publishing Group LLC
President James Buckley Jr.
Designer Tom Carling, carlingdesign.com

For WWE
Director, Home Entertainment & Books
Dean Miller
Photo Department
Frank Vitucci, Joshua Tottenham, Jamie Nelsen,
and Kevin Caldwell
Legal Lauren Dienes-Middlen

First American Edition, 2009
11 10 9 8 7 6 5 4
Published in the United States by DK Publishing
375 Hudson Street, New York, New York 10014

DK books are available at special discounts when purchased in bulk
for sales promotions, premiums, fund-raising, or educational use.
For details, contact: DK Publishing Special Markets,
375 Hudson Street, New York, New York 10014
SpecialSales@dk.com

A catalog record for this book is available
from the Library of Congress.

ISBN: 978-0-7566-5387-3 (Paperback)
ISBN: 978-0-7566-5388-0 (Hardcover)

Printed and bound by Lake Book.

The publisher would like to thank the following for their kind
permission to reproduce their photographs:
All photos courtesy WWE Entertainment, Inc.
All other images © Dorling Kindersley
For further information see: www.dkimages.com

Discover more at
www.dk.com

slammed WWE Champion JBL to the mat! Cena then landed on top of JBL, pinning his shoulders to the mat. The referee counted—1-2-3! The match was over! John Cena's lifelong dream came true. He was the new WWE Champion!

WWE championships come from hard work and a long journey. Where did John Cena's amazing journey begin?

John Cena grew up in the small town of West Newbury, Massachusetts. As a kid, he loved sports, hip-hop music, and watching WWE. His favorite WWE Superstars were Hulk Hogan, Ultimate Warrior, and Shawn Michaels. He watched their matches on TV.

Hulk Hogan

John dressed in hip-hop fashion.
He loved music, and he made up
his own lyrics and songs about
freedom. Being a young rebel in a
small town wasn't always popular.

He was not liked by
the other kids, who
were more into
hard rock.
They teased
him, which
only made him
more of a rebel.

Shawn Michaels

When Cena turned 15, he found a new passion. It would stop the teasing, and it would change his life forever. He began working out at the gym and developing himself as a bodybuilder.

Cena was also a very good student. He applied to 60 colleges and 58 accepted him! He picked Springfield College in Massachusetts.

GaryHood

He made the school's football team as an offensive lineman. He was a Division III All-American and the team's captain. He also earned a degree in exercise physiology (fizz-ee-OHL-oh-jee). He learned more about how the human body works. This helped when he joined WWE.

In 2000, Cena went to California to try a career as a bodybuilder. Competing in WWE was the furthest thing from his mind. He just wanted to build his body.

Then, while working at a gym, he heard about classes at Ultimate Pro Wrestling. Those who did well there could move onto WWE. Cena remembered his WWE heroes.

Cena's Stats and Stuff
- Name: John Cena
- Height: 6'1", Weight: 240 lbs.
- From: Newbury, Mass.
- Finishing Move: "Attitude Adjustment"

He decided to give it a shot. From
the first moment, he was hooked!

Cena learned everything he could about being a WWE Superstar. He quickly moved to the top of his class. Within a year he had caught the eye of WWE officials. They signed him to a contract and sent him to Ohio Valley Wrestling. That's where many future WWE Superstars trained.

At Ohio Valley Wrestling, in 2001, John really learned his stuff.

He impressed his teachers with his body, his strength, and his exciting energy. In June 2002, he took a step he could never have dreamed of as a kid. John Cena became a WWE Superstar.

Cena's first WWE matches were on *SmackDown*. His first costume was an old sports jersey and pair of sneakers. His first opponents were Superstars Kurt Angle, Chris

Jericho, Undertaker, Edge, and future WWE Hall-of-Famer Eddie Guerrero.

He picked up the first of his many nicknames. He was called "The Doctor of Thuganomics." He also created several signature moves with colorful names, such as the Attitude Adjustment and the Five-Knuckle Shuffle. Cena would use all these these moves to win!

Cena's first really huge WWE moment came at *WrestleMania XX* in March, 2004. That day he beat the man known as "The World's

Largest Athlete," the 7-foot-tall, 500-pound Big Show. Cena became the WWE United States Champion.

In 2005, he beat JBL at *WrestleMania 21*. That clinched his first WWE Championship. His dream had come true. He had reached the top of the WWE world.

Also in 2005, another dream came true. Cena was part of a tag team with two of his WWE heroes: Shawn Michaels and Hulk Hogan.

Cena spent the first part of
2006 defending his WWE
Championship around the world.
One of his toughest
matches came at
WrestleMania 22

in Chicago. There he battled Triple H. Cena won with his patented STF submission hold.

Later that year, Cena lost the title to Edge, who took him down with his trademark Spear. Cena had held the title for 280 days. This tied him with JBL as the longest title holder in nearly 20 years.

Cena's WWE Championship History
- 2 World Heavyweight Championships
- 2 World Tag Team Championships
- 3 WWE Championships
- 3 WWE United States Championships
- 2008 *Royal Rumble* Winner

Just three weeks after losing the title, Cena was back on top. He regained the WWE Championship, beating Edge at the *Royal Rumble* in Toronto, Canada.

The two Superstars battled on and off throughout the year. Their toughest match may have been at *Unforgiven 2006*. In a Tables, Ladders & Chairs Match, Cena showed his awesome strength. He tossed Edge off a 16-foot ladder, through two tables! They remain enemies to this day!

With his great success, Cena's
army of fans continued to grow.
His fans began calling themselves
the "Chain Gang." That fan
group earned Cena another
nickname: "The Chain Gang
Commander."

At *WrestleMania 23*, in 2007, Cena took on one of his childhood heroes, WWE legend Shawn Michaels. This famous figure was known as the "Heartbreak Kid" and the "Showstopper."

In a show-stopping move of his own, Cena sped to the match in Detroit in a sleek black Ford

Mustang. Then he defeated Michaels in front of 80,000 screaming fans at

Ford Field to keep his WWE
Championship. After that match,
both Cena and Michaels had
newfound respect for each other.

As his success grew, the list of challengers to Cena's crown kept getting longer. Next up was WWE Superstar Randy Orton. During his battle with Orton, Cena was injured for the first time in his

WWE career. Orton, known as "The Viper," hit Cena with his finishing move, called "the RKO," causing the injury.

Cena was forced to give up his WWE Championship while he recovered from his injury. Healed and rested, John Cena made his return to the ring at the 2008 *Royal Rumble* at Madison Square Garden.

That night, with his Chain Gang rooting him on, Cena took on Triple H. He won the match by throwing Triple H right over the top rope of the WWE ring! The crowd went crazy. "The Champ" was back in the house.

Next up for Cena was the huge celebration of *WrestleMania*'s 25th anniversary in April, 2009.

That night, Cena won his second World Heavyweight Championship. He showed his amazing strength to

win the match. He picked up *both*
Big Show and Edge, and slammed
them to the mat!

Today, John Cena continues to battle the WWE's most infamous Superstars. Whether he's competing on *Raw* or *SmackDown*, Cena never backs down from a challenge. He never gives up. Superstars like Chris Jericho, The Great Khali, Ted DiBiase, and The Miz have been on the receiving end of Cena's power in the ring.

Cena sometimes teams with his friends, such as Batista,

CM Punk, Rey Mysterio, Cryme Tyme, or Jeff Hardy. But whenever Cena is in the ring, WWE villains must beware of this powerful force of nature.

John Cena is more than just a WWE Superstar. In 2004, Cena was in the *Tribute to the Troops* show. Cena, along with many other WWE Superstars, traveled to the Middle East where they spent time with U.S. soldiers. He also works for the Make-A-Wish Foundation, helping to grant wishes for children with life-threatening illnesses.

Cena released his own rap album and has starred in two movies, *The Marine* and *12 Rounds*.

A champion in and out of the
ring, John Cena lives by three
ideals that have guided him
throughout his life: Hustle,
Loyalty, and Respect. He's a
Superstar any way you look at it.

John Cena Facts

- When John Cena beat WWE Champion JBL at *WrestleMania 21*, he proudly announced, "The Champ is here."

- John Cena's rap album, *You Can't See Me*, hit number 15 on the charts and has sold over 500,000 copies.

- WWE Chairman Vince McMahon once said, "John Cena was born to be WWE Champion."

- A car fan, John Cena's very first car was a 1983 Cadillac Coupe de Ville.

DK READERS

Level 2

Dinosaur Dinners
Fire Fighter!
Bugs! Bugs! Bugs!
Slinky, Scaly Snakes!
Animal Hospital
The Little Ballerina
Munching, Crunching, Sniffing,
    and Snooping
The Secret Life of Trees
Winking, Blinking, Wiggling,
    and Waggling
Astronaut: Living in Space
Twisters!
The Story of Pocahontas
Horse Show
Survivors: The Night the Titanic Sank
Eruption! The Story of Volcanoes
The Story of Columbus
Journey of a Humpback Whale
Amazing Buildings
Sniffles, Sneezes, Hiccups, and Coughs
Let's Go Riding
I Want to Be a Gymnast

Starry Sky
Earth Smart: How to Take Care
    of the Environment
Water Everywhere

Telling Time
A Trip to the Theater
Journey of a Pioneer
Inauguration Day
Power Rangers: Great Adventures
Star Wars: Journey Through Space
Star Wars: A Queen's Diary
Star Wars: Annakin in Action
Star Wars: R2-D2 and Friends
Meet the X-Men
¡Insectos! en español
Astronauta: La Vida in Espacio en
    español

Level 3

Spacebusters: The Race to the Moon
Beastly Tales
Shark Attack!
Titanic
Invaders from Outer Space
Movie Magic
Plants Bite Back!
Bermuda Triangle
Tiger Tales
Zeppelin: The Age of the Airship
Spies
Disasters at Sea
The Story of Anne Frank
Abraham Lincoln: Lawyer, Leader,
    Legend
George Washington: Soldier, Hero,
    President
Crime Busters
Extreme Sports
Spiders' Secrets
The Big Dinosaur Dig
Space Heroes: Amazing Astronauts
The Story of Chocolate
Solo Sailing
School Days Around the World

Polar Bear Alert!
Welcome to China
My First Ballet Recital
Ape Adventures
Amazing Animal Journeys
Greek Myths
Fantastic Four: The World's Greatest
    Superteam
Fantastic Four: Evil Adversaries
Star Wars: Star Pilot
Star Wars: I Want to Be a Jedi
Star Wars: The Story of Darth Vader
Star Wars: Yoda in Action!
Marvel Heroes: Amazing Powers
The X-Men School
Wolverine: Awesome Powers
Abraham Lincoln: Abogado, Líder,
    Leyenda en español
Al Espacio: La Carrera a la Luna
    en español

DK **Readers**

JOHN CENA

BRIAN SHIELDS